# Cherish Desire Singles:

# Intensity

## The Complete Five Part Series
## featuring Danielle

Written by

## Max D

brought to you by Cherish Desire

# DEDICATION

This book is dedicated to all the folks who survived working for NCR.

I thought things were confusing and bad enough, and then the AT&T acquisition proved how much worse it could be.

# CONTENTS

# Erotic Themes

This book is intended for mature audiences. Cherish Desire books contain erotica adventures featuring intense sexual situations including alternative lifestyles, perverse pleasures, and supernatural lust.

"Intensity 1 (A Danielle Story)" themes: MF, Object Insertion (Balfour Retractor), Bondage & Restraints, Implied Exhibitionism (Photo, Video), Implied Stretching, Implied Vaginal Penetration

"Intensity 2 (A Danielle Story)" themes: MF, Vaginal Penetration, Stretching, Object Insertion (Balfour Retractor), Bondage & Restraints

"Intensity 3 (A Danielle Story)" themes: MF, Vaginal Penetration, Stretching, Object Insertion (Balfour Retractor), Bondage & Restraints, Exhibitionism (Photo)

"Intensity 4 (A Danielle Story)" themes: MF, Object Insertion (Balfour Retractor), Stretching, Female Masturbation, Fingering, Vaginal Sex, Vaginal Penetration

"Intensity 5 (A Danielle Story)" themes: MF, Vaginal
& Oral Sex, Female Masturbation, Fingering, Vaginal
& Anal Penetration, Double Penetration, Implied
Stretching

# "Intensity 1 (A Danielle Story)"
## written by Max D

Featuring the Danielle and Ronin

*"Intensity 1 (A Danielle Story)" themes:* MF, Object Insertion (Balfour Retractor), Bondage & Restraints, Implied Exhibitionism (Photo, Video), Implied Stretching, Implied Vaginal Penetration

Danielle took a deep breath while trying to still her beating heart. Nothing really changed. She was on her forearms and shins with a loop of rope cruelly strapping her knees to her elbows. Danielle's wrists and ankles were held in place by velcro straps clipped to horizontal parachute nylon looping around the mattress. In such a precarious situation, it was no comfort that the bindings kept her legs and arms a bit wider than shoulder width apart. She was prevented from tipping completely forward by a cushion that fitted against her collarbone and stabilised her torso without pushing at her throat. A length of rope looped around her thighs where they met her pelvis

1

and was hooked overhead to keep her pussy and ass pointed up and out.

She'd been like this for several minutes, and blood was rushing to her head. Ronin had applied a cool creamy lubricant to her openings and then left the room. Initially it just felt slimy, but then it started to tingle. Eventually, she realized everything was numb from her tailbone to her clitoris. Danielle couldn't say when that happened with any certainty. The restraints were awkward. The bindings dug into the backs of her knees and inside of her elbows. Danielle was distracted by how moving to balance her weight meant working within the constraints of the bondage Ronin had applied to her body. Which definitely raised question in her mind about why he had put her in this position.

Naked. Bound. Exposed. In general, Danielle was frustrated and bored. Nothing was happening, and this wasn't even all that fun.

When Ronin came back in, Danielle asked him what he intended to do.

"First I'm going to stop you from talking," he replied quietly. "And then I'm going to give you something to take your mind off of thinking."

Danielle may have said something else as well. Ronin didn't pay attention. He took out a ball gag wettened with flavoured vodka, and he put worked it into her mouth. Danielle let him do so without fighting. She'd learned ball gags were something far more comfortable to get used to if she didn't piss

"Intensity 1 (A Danielle Story)"

Ronin off and make him force it past her teeth. And the vodka wasn't a bad touch. Probably Grey Goose with just enough fruit flavor to take the edge off the rubber taste without ruining the scent that she enjoyed.

While Danielle worked her jaw to get used to the ball gag, Ronin took out a latex wrap. Dark in colour and cut like a scarf, it fit very easily around her head. Warming and stretching it within his hands and fingers, Ronin used the wrap to blindfold Danielle. Her fine red hair streamed out from underneath the dark latex in the back. It largely covered her forehead, and her narrow nose and flaring nostrils peeked out from underneath the smooth latex in the front. As secondary benefit, the latex covered Danielle's ears so any sounds reaching her were muffled. And the redhead did love the smell of latex. Her deep breaths produced slow writhing within her bondage as she inhaled the strong fragrance of fetish fantasies. Danielle senses expanded, increasing her awareness of her body and his presence, even while her eyes and ears adjusted to the descent of partial darkness and quiet.

Ronin moved behind Danielle, framing her within his mind's lens, and looked around the room. He repositioned two lamps to provide the best possible illumination of all of Danielle's assets. Her gymnastic build - slight but well formed - and her clearly displayed femininity, greased and slightly open, glowed warmly under the lamps attention. The pale skin with the hint of freckles on the arms and shoulders reflected the light as he directed the lamp to remove any overt gaps in coverage. The natural curves and line of her body shone in their own right once he angled the lamp away enough to allow shadows to gather close along the edges of her form to provide contrast and depth. Satisfied with the scene, he stepped over to the closet and brought out two tripods with cameras attached.

The first camera he positioned looking at Danielle from an angle off her front right shoulder. It captured her latex wrapped face and hanging breasts as well as her bondage and the way her lower back curved upward to rise before launching into the understated curves of her up thrust bottom. The second camera was placed looking over his shoulder and focused on her openings and along the line of her backbone. It could see her prominent labia and the sunken depression of her anus as well as the straps holding her in position.

He started the cameras recording before lifting his tools from the end table strategically placed at the end of the bed. The video started with clanking sounds of the spoons on the steel retractors, the stainless steel rattling when lifted into position behind Danielle's bound body, and his strong biceps flexed with restrained power. As the curved spoons were fit against her flesh, it became clear that Ronin intended to use the retractors to fully open her sex.

It hadn't begun like this. This is what Danielle and Ronin had to work up to over time.

# "Intensity 2 (A Danielle Story)"

## written by Max D

Featuring the Danielle and Ronin

*"Intensity 2 (A Danielle Story)" themes:* MF, Vaginal Penetration, Stretching, Object Insertion (Balfour Retractor), Bondage & Restraints

Danielle leaned back in her chair and stretched with her hands over her head. She was still tired from going out Saturday night, and now she was trying to catch up on work for Monday. "At least it's raining out," she muttered to herself while looking over her laptop at the rain pummeling her deck window.

A part of her wished, deep down, that she was out in the storm. Danielle was held in place, restrained by her work and her commitments to some vague notion of achievement in a career, yet there was a time when she would have stripped down and stepped out there to enjoy the summer rain soaking her within a few minutes and then getting her off with its relentless fury. The sheets of pummeling raindrops driven by alternating windy gusts would have battered and caressed her, and Danielle would have felt connected to the storm itself, taking meaning from its unrelenting demands on her body, while she spread her thighs and let mother nature project her soaked fury at her sensitive labia.

Instead, she shook her head and forced herself to focus on the task at hand. Danielle swept her fine red hair back, centered her herself with a deep breath and an adjustment to her posture, and considered the list of things jotted down on her stenopad. There were a dozen more status reports and requirement documents to review and reconcile. Then it would be time to make some salad for lunch, allow herself a break to do some cardio, and update her progress.

Curling a hand around her mug of cooling tea, she clicked send with her mouse to clear the current set of revisions and recommendations. Starting a new email, Danielle began to dive into another cluster of documents related to requirements lacking prioritization, flouting template standards, and missing indexing for testing team validation.

~~~

Sitting within his home office, immersed within the soft whir of cooling fans pierced by the subtle high frequency whine of multiple CPUs in various computer cases, Ronin pulled up an intranet company directory and keyed in her name. His current project
~~~

suffered from all the usual ailments associated with bad management: poor conception, limited knowledge, and unguided execution. And now, on a Sunday, he had a new nuisance to deal with. Someone was systematically reviewing all the requirement specifications previously agreed to and signed. That someone was blasting out revisions and commentary to both internal and client leadership teams. He'd already received multiple quick notes asking if he was responsible for what was happening. On Monday morning when the execs who really did take weekends off caught up, there'd be an explosion of consequences which he would need to mitigate and manage.

The intranet slowly spun, hunting down his unwitting adversary. His fingers pushed hard against his forehead and over his sparsely covered scalp. As much as Ronin knew that this was just another example of why this entire project should be reset, he was very close to final delivery on a handful of key items. He'd only been pulled in because the project was in crisis and revenue was threatened. With those milestones in place, he bought breathing room for follow on leads and Ronin could easily justify moving on to a project with far less drama and idiocy. He didn't need the distraction of losing a week to arguments over emails from an uninformed consultant. He definitely didn't need that to trigger new moving targets for delivery.

A profile pulled up, the usual default information provided by the HR backend systems, and he sighed.

No matter how often it was explained to people that their profile was their brand, people simply ignored how critical providing their real details were to colleagues around the world. His mind was already racing ahead, evaluating how the requirements feedback could undermine his project team, the innumerable replanning sessions and client meetings which would be needed to point out that the signed off requirements were the best that could be a pulled together given the client's lack of understanding and minimal interest in the program despite substantial political pressure, and what people he should prioritize speaking to one-on-one before things built up to a crisis during the Monday afternoon exec call.

He clicked around. Went deeper, into the project and management views, and was rewarded when he found a team specific intranet page identifying each person involved and their roles. The woman's corporate photo came up alongside a list of her credentials, past projects, and former managers. Group photos at the current client site, celebrating some internal only achievement based on the lack of any client presence, were discouraging. Most of her close colleagues were comfortable living off the revenue generated by others while pretending to be advising. Her mobile phone number was listed along with other contact information, but he fought the urge to call her at home given it was Sunday.

Instead, he sent an email introducing himself and asking for a meeting first thing Monday morning. On the list of items to discuss, he included "Contributing to improved requirements." The emphasis was intentional, on Danielle not just commenting on specifications but actually following through and revising them, and her response to that would determine what the strategy he adopted when confronted by leadership about the incongruences and negative feedback the consultant had tossed into everyone's lap.

Sometimes, an email and a request for a meeting was all it took to stop people from accidentally sabotaging their careers. Ronin figured that his request might at least make this woman pause and consider her objectives carefully. If it didn't, then he'd see if her energy and input could be channeled into actually doing requirements gathering for the next project phase. Setting aside something awkwardly familiar about her appearance, he got the impression that she was younger consultant straight out of a degree and bootcamp program. Her corporate project team profile picture presented her with orange-red hair pulled back tightly in a bun. Once she was bogged down and dealing with the client on a daily basis, she'd have no opportunity to derail his delivery schedule.

While making a note to himself and copying her details to it, Ronin noticed her number and office assignment were local to him, but it didn't really matter at the moment.

~~~

Danielle finished three more requirements
~~~

documents, carefully saving them and then uploading them to the shared version control repository for the project in a new review folder she'd started on Thursday. She opened her email draft to clean it up and add links before sending out the status and comments on the marked up documents, and was surprised to see she had gotten a new email in the last forty-five minutes.

The sender was a person she knew was associated with the program, but she couldn't connect the name with a face. Danielle skimmed his email, got a clear sense that he was not a happy person, and then re-read the email to make sure she didn't miss anything. When she took his email address and copied it to her corporate instant messenger window, he showed up as available.

It made sense to ask in her mind. "Hello. Who are you on the NUI project?"

The response took a minute. Ronin hated being interrupted by instant messenger, and he had to save everything he was working on before switching applications. "Delivery for Phase 1 integration. You must be new. I didn't recognize your photo as someone working with us on requirements and analysis."

"No. I've been working on this for two months."

"Then you should probably meet with my team lead and I as well as Jon Bernette and Kelly Thomas who did the requirements you are now modifying."

"I'm just doing QA on these. I don't have time to

meet with anyone."

"If you don't work with Jon and Kelly then it's not a good idea to add commentary on their deliverables *after* the customer has already signed off on them."

Danielle was used to this. Her job was clear: Make certain that the standards for projects were adhered to. This put her in conflict with most delivery teams because their primary objectives focused on meeting delivery timeframes. "These documents don't meet our standards." She wanted to say more, but anything further might show up in emails later.

Ronin laughed out loud - a harsh barking laugh that competed with the drumming rain on his home office window - and replied, "Ok." It took him three minutes to send out an email to the requirements and business analysis team leads, Jon and Kelly, introducing Danielle and encouraging them to leverage her clear alignment with standards to assist with the quality of phase two requirements. "Good luck!" he sent after that and signed off.

If she had any question of how unhappy Ronin was then her doubts were removed when Danielle saw him end their chat and then received the email he sent to multiple people. Her job wasn't to support the requirements team, and it definitely did not involve her getting into the middle of the delivery process. She shook her head in frustration and decided to call it a day. Monday would be the start of another busy week, and she was hungry.

~~~

She bit down a little harder on the smooth rubber ball in her mouth.  A wide breathing tube straight through the center of the ball gag allowed Danielle to crush it slightly while still inhaling air.  She could feel pulling and tugging on her skin - unnatural sensations since everything else was numb.  It wasn't pain per se, but it was accompanied by an urge to pull away and itch and scratch at the spot where her flesh was being stretched.

Ronin applied a hand on her buttock to steady her. Danielle was tied to minimize her ability to move, but too much of a rocking motion would change how the retractor fit into her pussy.  He continued to slowly ease the wide steel spoons between Danielle's pink labia, using one hand to push them deeper while he held her ass in place.

The Balfour retractor wasn't heavy, but the spoons that went into Danielle's pussy had curves that fit best at just the right depth before being slowly ratcheted apart using the cross piece.  The arms holding the spoons were a good five inches long, which also made managing the entire apparatus with only one hand an interesting challenge.  But Ronin was quite skilled at this from practice, and it only took him a few minutes to fit the steel spoons into position and then nudge the retractor open enough to stay in place while he moved his hand to the cross piece and snugged the thumbscrew.
~~~

"Intensity 2 (A Danielle Story)"

Danielle had come to him with a typical sexual history.  Boyfriends, some bigger than others, and a few vibrators that hadn't made much of an impact on her pussy's size.  Her compact build, the product of gymnastics when she was in high school and university, and petite five foot two inch frame meant her vagina had been uncomfortably forced open to handle the bigger cocks she'd fucked.  But she never alluded to anything more than just that - cocks up to an inch and a half wide - and her vibes were that size or smaller.

The Balfour retractor made its usual metal on metal noises while Ronin took her pussy well beyond those tiny beginnings again.  Danielle's stubby labia pulled back, drawn to the sides by the metal spoons, and there was visible clenching and contractions occurring just beyond the end of the spoons.  It took a little more stretching, sliding the one arm of the retractor along the crosspiece to spread the curved stainless steel prongs further apart, before Ronin could see the hollowing cavern glistening with lube and arousal within Danielle's pussy.

He paused there, as he always did, and leaned in close so Danielle could hear his muffled voice through the dark blue latex wrap that covered her eyes and ears.  "Opened to four fingers to warm up. Now for the real stretch."

Danielle exhaled loudly, trying to shape words around the ball gag, and then projected her voice as best she could without being able to properly form the sounds with her lips and teeth.

Ronin laughed. "I need to make it bigger? Why yes, yes I do." He kissed Danielle's bare back. "Just for you I'll make your opening as big as I can." There was obvious joy in his voice as Ronin said this. Danielle didn't need to see his smile to know it was there.

Then he began to work the retractor arm along the crosspiece. The arm's thumbscrew loosened so he could grip the steel bar and push the arm with his thumb. He used his other fingers to lightly stroke and caress Danielle's numb clit and labia, enjoying the fleshy feeling of the skin while it started to become engorged with blood despite how he was stretching it. Ronin spoke out loud, narrating the progress as he felt Danielle squirming a bit from the odd tugging sensations on her labia and the skin of her abdomen and inner thighs.

"Two inches." He pushed further, being delicate but firm so the retractor arm didn't slide unevenly and the spoons didn't pinch her labia at an angle.

"Two and a half inches."

Ronin could now easily see four inches deep into the oval tunnel of Danielle's pussy. The initial ring of tissue near her opening was pale and pink, and then there was a transition point - the second ring inside of her vagina - where the walls were a deep red and quivered with each beat of Danielle's pulse.

"Three inches." Now the round flesh snout of Danielle's cervix was coming into view. The colour was a rich pink with deep red striations like linear clouds circling a tornado funnel. The distinct doughnut shaped ring around the fingertip-sized opening of her cervix was much brighter red.

Tightening the thumb screw so the arm was locked in place on the crosspiece steel bar, Ronin took a break to run his hands over Danielle's buttocks and thighs. He lightly kneaded and massaged her tense muscles, willing them to relax with the drumming of his fingers and the heat of his palms. Then he stroked over her flesh, pressing up from Danielle's buttocks, along her lower back, and sliding all the way to her shoulder blades. His hands made slow oval circuits, coming up on either side of her spine and then down along the sides of her rib cage. When Danielle stopped trembling, he simply and loudly asked, "More?"

Danielle's breathy response was obvious. "Please."

He added a few squirts of silicon lube to his left hand, and stroked it generously over Danielle's open sex. He knew she hated the word, but he used it anyway. "Anything less than this is just a pussy," he began solely for Danielle's benefit. She shook her head, anticipating his comment but not saying anything. After wiping his slippery hand off on a dry section of towel without much success, Ronin released the thumbscrew and began pushing the retractor beyond the three inch mark on the steel bar. "Now you have a cunt."

Danielle wanted to hear that. She wanted to hear

it loudly and clearly. Instead, she heard it from a distance, like listening to sounds carried across a lake or deep in a cave, due to the muffling effect of the stretched latex wrap covering her ears. She struggled, slightly bucking her hips with frustration, and sensed Ronin hesitate. If only she could make him understand. Choosing her words carefully, knowing the ball gag made everything difficult to say and comprehend, Danielle tried to ask for him to take the blindfold off.

The sounds were unrecognizable as words, but that made them even more curious to Ronin. He tightened the thumbscrew in place, and then moved to Danielle's side. He took his time to slowly and carefully undo the ball gag strap, and then he gripped the ball gag with a finger in the hollow center and eased it out of Danielle's mouth. "What's that?"

It took a moment of moving her lips and her tongue to get her mouth working properly again. Ronin patiently waited to hear what Danielle wanted. He was surprised when she asked for him to remove the blindfold.

Speaking loudly so she could hear him through the latex covering her ears, Ronin asked, "And why would I do that? If I take off your blindfold then you can see, you can hear, you will have to face what you came here for. You are the one who asked to be kept in the dark…"

Danielle once again chose her words very carefully. "You always said there would come a time when I would accept this is what I wanted." She took a deep breath, feeling the odd pinching sensation of the Balfour retractor arms sagging and tugging on her thighs while pulling on her pussy opening. "I want to hear you say it..."

He didn't respond. He simply started unwrapping the latex sheet, careful not to get lube or catch and pull on Danielle's fine hair, and removed it. Then he leaned in close to her, her ears and cheeks warm from being covered up, and let his words brush over her ear lobe. "Are you ready to accept why you are here?"

She moaned and shivered from the tingling sensation of his breath on her warm ear and the pulsing wetness within her pussy. Ronin returned to the retractor, gently adjusted it, satisfied himself that the silicon lube was still keeping her labia wet, and began to stretch her further. "As I said," he began in warm tones, "anything less than three inches is just a pussy." Ronin felt the resistance of Danielle's sex press against the retractor arm and overcame it.

"Three and a quarter." He paused, let the measurement sink in, then continued. "There," he said with quiet satisfaction. "Now you have a cunt."

# "Intensity 3 (A Danielle Story)"
## written by Max D

Featuring the Danielle and Ronin

*"Intensity 3 (A Danielle Story)" themes:* MF, Vaginal Penetration, Stretching, Object Insertion (Balfour Retractor), Bondage & Restraints, Exhibitionism (Photo)

Danielle watched as her schedule for Monday fell apart. Her manager was waiting for her when she arrived, and he had two printed out emails in hand. His false smile didn't nearly cover how vexed he was, and Danielle knew it was all because of that jerk on Sunday. In half an hour, she had been reassigned to work and support Kelly's team making sure that JAD workshop documents and new requirements were meeting quality objectives, and all her work on the existing documentation was being abandoned.

After meeting with Kelly Thomas, it got worse. The Phase 2 Requirements Lead was in a rush to finish the client interviews and had been short staffed for a month.  With just a hallway conversation, she assigned everything that hadn't been done to Danielle, welcomed her to the team, and then headed off to meetings for the rest of the day.  Danielle didn't know where to start and had nobody to ask since most of the team was still en route to the client site.

She was about to throw up her hands and melt down when an older man with close cropped hair and broad shoulders walked into the workroom.  He was average height and didn't seem important, but the other three people in the requirements room immediately stopped what they were doing and the nearest one reached out to shake his hand.  Convinced this must be one of the client executives, Danielle fixed her blouse and turned to be introduced.

"And you must be Danielle.  Nice to see you are getting situated," he smiled and offered his hand.

Danielle was caught off guard since it was impossible to believe that anyone on the client team knew she was now on Kelly's team, much less transitioned that morning to work on Kelly's team. "Yes... yes, I am.  And you are?"

He chuckled and let go of her hand.  "I'm Ronin.  Welcome to the delivery team.  Based on how thorough your work has been, Kelly and I are excited to see that energy poured into getting Phase 2 ahead of the curve."  Then he was called back to the hallway by someone, and with a "See you later," he vanished into another discussion.

~~~

At lunch, Danielle's manager explained why he was grumpy in the morning. Apparently, Kelly's team had been trying to get two additional business requirements people for the past few months, and Ronin and Kelly made a compelling argument to the PMO that reassigning Danielle to one of those roles would make a big difference. Instead of her auditing and marking up signed deliverables for internal reasons, Danielle could now help create better deliverables that would improve the client's satisfaction as well as bring in the project timelines.

He shook his head. "After that there was nothing I could do. You've always worked hard and done excellent work, and that was used as an argument for why you should be embedded in Kelly's team. Initially two options were presented, and this was definitely the better of the two."

"What was the other option?"

"Working directly with Ronin's team and dealing with gaps between customer statements in workshops and requirements, and feedback coming in from testing and user acceptance. It seems the requirements were definitely not well understood by the client line of business teams, so Ronin is running into a lot of defects that can be traced to disagreements within the client team on how some business functionality should be handled. You would
~~~

have been stuck in a high stress spot trying to run interference between the client groups while matching joint testing to incomplete requirements. Even Ronin thought that role would be a bit of a stretch for you, but given your detailed understanding of the requirements based on your reviews, he pointed out you would be a knowledgeable resource that could help finish out the testing and promotion of Phase 1."

Looking at her caesar salad, Danielle shook her head. "I'd rather not work with Ronin if I can help it…"

She was about to say more when her manager cut her off sharply enough to make her look up. "Ronin is someone you should get to know better. You always talk about how you want to do more and want to broaden your career. That guy has done all that and has experience you won't find very often. I can only do so much, but people like Ronin don't play by the usual rules and act like free agents. Yet they will always have work, and they get involved in some really intense situations." He looked at Danielle and read the sour expression on her face. "Just to put it in context, because I know you don't believe me, Phase 1 delivery was believed to be six months off schedule. Ronin got involved about the same time as you, maybe a couple of weeks earlier, and had to sort out the requirements, specifications, and put together a delivery team that knew the technology. He had help, but he also had a lot of the program folks angry at him for pointing out all the prerequisites and dependencies that they didn't even have on plans.

Rumour has it, and I'm sure it's true, he has vacation scheduled for next month so he intends to deliver Phase 1 early so he can go on holiday and leave the project."

Danielle nodded - not really following.

Her manager just laughed. "So now Phase 1 is a month ahead of schedule, just because he wants to go to Europe and not be bothered by phone calls. He hacked the scope down so tight that the client was completely caught off guard and demanded a contractual review. PMO grudgingly had to point out that Ronin had already identified numerous client responsibilities and dependencies that were not in place, and the client would need to sign change requests across the board just to get anything within the year. It was really ugly for a couple of weeks, yet Ronin is still here and his vacation is still going to happen. That says a lot about what someone can do when they don't care about the consequences."

~~~

At three and a half inches, Ronin was looking deep into the smooth red and pink walls of Danielle's cunt. He paused for a moment and added a bit of menthol cream to Danielle's clit. The slow burn would be dulled down by the numbing anesthetic, but it would be good to start getting her sensitive skin used to the cream and the extra stimulation.

"Three and three quarters." The retractor arm was becoming quite difficult to move as Danielle's tight
~~~

opening fought against being spread any further. Ronin asked her if she was willing to go on, projecting his voice clearly so she had could feel the intensity of the question, and Danielle immediately said "Yes" despite feeling out of breath. Using both hands, he had to muscle the retractor arm along the steel cross piece, feeling the remaining silicon lube on his left hand making his grip slippery. Finally he compromised, holding the fixed retractor arm with his left hand and pulling the other arm away from it with his right hand. He awkwardly worked the thumbscrew from the side, and then tightened it more thoroughly when he didn't need to keep pressure on both arms.

"Four inches." Danielle's cunt mouth was distorted in a wide diamond shape. Her clitoris was a small bead exposed by tightly stretched skin pulled toward the retractor spoons. Her labia were white where the steel spoons held them back, and the ridge of pelvis bone was clearly protruding above and below the dull metal. Looking into Danielle, the line of her inner thigh seemed to continue into a deep dark recess, the pinker flesh of her cervix fixed in the middle with dark reds proceeding further into her body on either side.

Ronin picked up a wet wipe and slowly cleaned off each finger on his left hand. Then, he used another wet wipe for his right hand and fingers. Finally, he used a third to make sure any juices or lube on his palms and the back of his hands were cleaned up. These discards joined a small pile on a towel set on the corner of the bed. With his hands clean, Ronin picked up his digital camera began to take photos.

"You do want to see your cunt, don't you?" he asked rhetorically as the flash went off; he adjusted settings, and then took another photo. "You wanted to hear, to see, to know why you've asked me to do this, right? Why you consented to come here twice a week and help me restrain you so you cannot stop your cunt from being stretched and satisfied... Why you need to be anesthetized so nothing prevents you from having a wonderful open cunt..."

He took photos looking directly into Danielle's gaping opening. When his flash didn't provide enough light, he paused to fetch a posable LED lamp and made sure the entire depth of Danielle's sex would show in the photos. "So now what, though? Now you have a cunt just like you asked for... Stretched four inches wide." He ran his hand over the tight curve of her ass cheek and then stroked her stretched labia with his finger tips. "Is your ass next? What's your plan now?" He chuckled. "What are your requirements?"

Danielle knew he was messing with her head. She hadn't asked for this, surely she hadn't planned it, and these weren't her requirements. They were his. She paused to consider carefully something Ronin had said when they met for lunch after his European vacation trip. "You said," she focused harder, "that you would never lie."

He smiled, still taking photos mostly for the psychological impact of doing so, and responded gently, "I'm telling the truth." He looked over her, the ropes holding her down and balancing Danielle on her knees and forearms. "You helped me pick out the ropes today. You told me what flavoured vodkas you liked. You even helped me size the blindfold you later asked me to take off. You come over, ring the door bell, and ask to come in. You even set the rules - though today you've broken them - saying you wanted to enjoy not seeing, not hearing, not knowing..."

Danielle saw the truth in everything Ronin said, yet there was so much more to why she was here. He was picking and choosing the facts he liked. "You... you told me I was too small..." she blurted out, looking for the underlying cause, struggling to establish her ground.

But Ronin had led Danielle to this slippery slope weeks ago when this all started. Had she done as he suggested at the time - simply walk away - then he wouldn't even know how she enjoyed the scent of rubber and latex never mind have an unobstructed view of her cunt and cervix. "Too small for me. I offered to introduce you to other men whom you might like. Men who would settle for your hot body and tight holes." He finished taking photos and set the camera on the bedside table. After a pause to consider his options, he continued, "I'm going to let you go, right now, and then you can decide what you want."

He started loosening the rope, careful to guide Danielle so when her balance shifted she didn't fall to one side. When he was done, Ronin released the clips affixed to her wrists and ankles. The velcro strap looping her elbows to her knees came apart with a loud ripping sound. Then he eased Danielle up, and carefully lowered her down while keeping her from twisting or yanking on the Balfour Retractor.

Without a word he scooped up dirty towels and the pile of wet wipes and took them away. He returned with a tall mirror he placed so it was leaning against the bed facing Danielle's thighs and pelvis. Then he got into bed and stretched out on his back, his khaki trousers and tight black shirt in stark contrast with the rose red sheets.

"Don't look unless you are ready to accept this is what you wanted. I'll take it out in half an hour so I know the stretch is holding."

Danielle turned to him, suddenly careful when she felt the retractor dig into her thighs, and asked, "Why do you say I wanted this?"

He spoke to the ceiling with his head settling into the pillows. "You kept coming back. I may have told you what I considered necessary. But you were the one who came over the next day after that. You could have walked away, or you could have simply kept things platonic, but instead you offered yourself for me to strip down, to bathe and wash, and then to restrain so you could be stretched and opened."

Ronin was leaving a lot out, but again Danielle had to admit to the truth in the statements as well. "So now you want me to tell you what to do next?"

"It was hard work to turn your tight pussy into a cunt. I hope you are a bit less demanding in the future."

Whispering what she had really wanted, putting it in Ronin's words, took more effort than Danielle expected. "So am I open enough to fuck?"

Ronin judged Danielle's vulnerability and nodded his head. He turned toward her, and stroked a few fingers along her cheek to her temple. "I only fuck cunts, Danielle. Can you live with having a cunt for me to fuck?" He paused and brushed his hand along her arm. "I don't want to hurt you."

She paused, considering his attention and his gently spoken admission, and asked, "But wouldn't I only need to be three inches wide then? Don't you want more than that?"

He smiled as his fingers pushed a reddish curl back off her ear. "Do you know what you have once your cunt is wider than four inches?" He paused and enjoyed her slow head shake while her fingers reached down to trace the edge of the Balfour retractor. "Do you want to know?" He could see how she was drawn in and so very ready for the next step.

She waited for it. Needing to hear... but not wanting to. Her fingers could feel the heat of her distorted and stretched opening, and the slightest pressure on her skin caused her body to tingle and tremble despite the numbing anesthetic.

"A gaping hole."

# "Intensity 4 (A Danielle Story)"
## written by Max D

Featuring the Danielle and Ronin

*"Intensity 4 (A Danielle Story)" themes:* MF, Object Insertion (Balfour Retractor), Stretching, Female Masturbation, Fingering, Vaginal Sex, Vaginal Penetration

Danielle didn't per se meet with Ronin, but his presence was pervasive in the project environment. He could be seen working with the architect team and then driving PMO changes. He attended meetings, sometimes passively listening and seeming disconnected, and other times taking over the meeting agenda to address specific details that were being missed.

While some of the team felt uncomfortable around Ronin, it was clear he had a core of loyalists that felt his approach was turning the tide. And true to his word, he pushed hard to get his release into test and then handed the reins over to someone else before leaving for Germany.

It was the day before his trip that Danielle ended up sitting with Ronin one-on-one.

"How have you liked being in a role where you make a difference?" he asked her.

Danielle looked into Ronin's face. She expected some guile or at least a sense of dishonesty there. So many things had happened since he had orchestrated her reassignment to work under Kelly's team. Her own manager had been rolled off the project, along with the majority of the QA and audit staff. Yet she had been given accolades and recognition for her hard work and even been encouraged to consider making a permanent change over to a focused delivery team.

Sitting casually, brushing some stray red hair off her forehead, she felt Ronin was being open with her. So she responded in kind. "I look forward to making a difference for the firm, and that means shifting back to addressing systemic quality on multiple engagements."

He laughed. Matching her, he leaned back in his seat and used a single finger to push an imaginary hair off his brow. Every movement was calculated, intentional, and spoke of extreme control. "Well, I tried. You're too good to be wasted double-checking other people's work, but at least you got some hands on experience so now you understand the need for streamlined approaches as well as methodology deviations." Even his language was shaped to match Danielle's.

"Don't..." she started and stopped short when he gave her a wolfish grin. "What? Aren't we waiting for Kelly?"

"I asked Kelly to set this meeting up. As everyone will find out over the next day or so, I won't intentionally be coming back to this client. I did what I could, and now it's up to the usual suspects to keep things running." He gestured toward her. "The question is whether you prefer to stay in place or to move on to the next firefight."

Danielle got it then, the openness and the humour on Ronin's face as well as his intentions. "Are you asking if I'll work for you?" she exhaled involuntarily, caught off guard with her surprise visibly showing, and studied the man sitting across from her. It took her a moment to recompose herself and cover up her shock.

"Perhaps. But my teams need quality while delivering. Each team is configured and built differently. I need someone who can consistently parse the contractual obligations, support me defining success, and then work through the innumerable problems with requirements and client input to get us to the real defining conditions and boundaries of the solution. You could do real well by staying here, but it will just be more of the same. You could also do well returning to Jeff's team on project audits, but that group is being downsized. We protected you here by making you fully billable, and I can't speak for when QA will come back in favour internally." He paused, looked Danielle over, and shrugged. "My teams hit the ground with little or no briefing, deal with the worst disasters and politics imaginable, and fix what everyone else says cannot be fixed. We are usually disliked and perceived as intruders - but, without us, multimillion dollar projects simply fall apart. You would be put to the test daily, but it will feel like you are really making a difference. What you learn in five years working in my teams is equivalent to twenty years or more of regular project work. Actually," he put his hand on the table and drummed his fingers thoughtfully, "other teams simply do not learn what my teams do. Their experiences are tightly limited by the scale of the problems they encounter. We deal with problems that change the future of companies and countries."

It took a minute for Danielle to let it settle in. She considered the various rumours and stories that Ronin told and people told about Ronin. "No." She didn't smile and didn't frown. Danielle tried to make her face as neutral as possible. It was never wise to turn down an offer without knowing what was next, but Danielle was confident that being in Ronin's orbit was not a good idea.

He smiled warmly and leaned back into his seat further. His body language was intentionally shaped to show no threat and no hostility. "Tell me why not."

"It's not what I want."

"Intensity 4 (A Danielle Story)"

"That may change over time.  Keep in touch. Enjoy this while it lasts, but when you are ready for more, call me for lunch and we'll talk."  Ronin spoke with confidence that suggested he could see the future very clearly.  It was that self confidence bordering on blatant arrogance that he depended on and which Danielle took as validation that she'd rather keep her distance.

He got up, and Danielle was struck by the effortless way he moved through the room.  As Ronin walked by her to leave, he stopped and turned.  His hand brushed hers, and he smiled down at Danielle. "Even if you just need some advice, reach out. Everything is always in motion, and, for someone as sharp as you, I'm willing to volunteer time to make sure you realize your potential."  Then he left, and Danielle was very much on her own in an unremarkable office to think about what had just happened.

Right down to the unexpected comfort of Ronin's touch and the reassuring tones in his voice.

~~~

Ronin was confident he had said enough.  He allowed Danielle time to think her way through the situation.  He hadn't pursued her intimately, but he certainly hadn't turned the good looking redhead away.  If all she really wanted was his approval, his satisfaction, and his interest in fucking her - then she
~~~

had achieved that. She had, at his suggestion, come over twice a week just for these exercise sessions. All because she had asked if he found her attractive, and he had responded with the qualifying statement that he preferred his lovers to be open rather than tight. Her methodical approach to this, combined with his straightforward outline of what could be done step by step, had brought them to this point.

Comfortably settled into his bed, Ronin made no motion, thus he could feel any movement by Danielle through the mattress and duvet. It was slow at first, and he had to resist a grin when it became obvious that Danielle was slowly pleasuring her numb cunt. In the still and quiet air of his bedroom, Danielle's slow stroking motions of her fingers became increasing obvious as she lifted her pelvis up to thrust against her fingers and her breathing became more and more excited.

Ronin doubted this was a show for him. Instead, he suspected that a repressed part of Danielle's sexuality was finally finding its way to the surface. This was the full admission that opening herself, bringing herself to be stretched and pulled open, was pleasurable and enjoyable no matter what beliefs Danielle had before. He didn't interrupt, didn't move, and didn't insert himself into her personal release.

It was enough for Ronin to enjoy basking within the glow of the moment, the sexual energy tingling within the room, and the scent of Danielle's sweet juices becoming more obvious as her cunt overheated and finally erupted in an orgasm that left her shuddering beside him.

Only then did Ronin move, running a hand along her arm and feeling Danielle's wet fingers gripping and squeezing his hand in hers. He turned to her, knowing she could only move so much with the Balfour retractor still embedded in her cunt, and kissed her forehead. That gentle and easily given acceptance ignited Danielle's passion and hunger. She awkwardly leveraged herself up and kissed Ronin's lips, and then let him lower her down to the pillow while kissing her back. Ronin positioned himself carefully so his thigh was between her legs but not touching the retractor, all while his kisses pressed firmly into her lips with his tongue lightly touching hers. He lifted up and delivered a string of light pecks and kisses over her cheek and nose.

He paused to breathe, to steal the air she exhaled, and then he asked her, "Would you like to feel me inside of you next?"

Danielle trembled as her body responded with a surge of lust before she could find the words to express her passions. Her open pussy gushed warm wetness all over her inner thighs. She was glad he didn't wait, glad he was already easing off his shirt, and, when she could form a coherent thought, all that came out was "Please..."

Ronin did his best to keep touching Danielle. His fingers on her skin as he lifted his shirt up with the other hand. His thigh against her thigh as he pulled his shirt over his head. His arm along her side as he pushed his trousers and boxers off. He had to get up, to move away from her to get a condom out of the bedside table drawer, but Danielle understood his intent and pulled him gently back by one arm. "It's safe," she said softly - her longing for his bare cock in her cunt conveyed in her pleading tones for him to not worry.

He nodded and shifted to sit by her knees. Ronin's fingers deftly manipulated the thumbscrew and arms of the retractor and cautiously brought the spoons together. He was worried about pinching or catching the stretched flesh of Danielle's labia and opening ring, but his deliberate and controlled motions minimized the risk and any discomfort.

His smile was broad and bright when he finally lifted the Balfour retractor out of Danielle's vagina. She didn't notice. Danielle had other things on her mind. Ronin set the retractor aside, the metal spoons and armature clicking and clanking, and then mounted her with easy confidence.

She felt his legs pushing hers apart like in a dream. When she opened her eyes, Ronin was right there, over top of her, and she took in the hair on his chest as well as the muscle definition across his shoulders and biceps while Ronin dipped his cock into her. Feeling the pressure between her thighs and the hint of penetration despite her anesthetized state, Danielle lifted her legs out and tucked her knees back a bit. Ronin was smiling now and he simply pushed all the way down into her sex. She sensed his cock, or rather the pressure of it, at the opening to her pussy. But deeper inside Danielle could definitely feel his swollen head and shaft stroking against her walls and g-spot. She wrapped her legs around his waist to encourage him deeper.

"Is this comfortable?" Ronin asked politely once he felt his pelvis firmly pressed against Danielle's wet hot labia. He was curious what she could feel.

Danielle rocked herself from side to side a bit, letting her hips spread naturally, and then ran her hands down Ronin's ribs to his buttocks. "Just take it slow," she said with lust in her voice. "I want this to last a really long time."

# "Intensity 5 (A Danielle Story)"

## written by Max D

Featuring the Danielle and Ronin

*"Intensity 5 (A Danielle Story)" themes:* MF, Vaginal & Oral Sex, Female Masturbation, Fingering, Vaginal & Anal Penetration, Double Penetration, Implied Stretching

There was a moment of shared silence between them, when the sound of her heart beating fast became a sudden storm within her ears, and then Danielle slowly exhaled as Ronin eased his cock into her sex.  Instead of feeling the pressure of his glans parting her labia, she sensed the path of his penetration based on the tender spots his manhood brushed against within her pussy.  It was... difficult. Danielle's eyes watered a bit, and her emotions bubbled to the surface.  Ronin quietly watched, his eyes locked on hers, and continued his downward thrust until the top of his quads pressed against her inner thighs.

"Intensity 5 (A Danielle Story)"

Her hand stroked Ronin's hip when he slowly slipped his cock back. When she squeezed tight and pulled on him, when Danielle admitted she wanted more, Ronin pushed back into her open wetness. His cock glided in and out. His slightly darker bare skin pressing against the rosy flush of the redhead's swollen lips. They moved in unison and carefully explored the sore spots and torn flesh of her stretched opening and soaked depths. The stainless steel retractor had forced Danielle's pussy mouth to yield to it's industrial strength, and, even a week later, there was no sign of her fleshy lips returning to the tight pucker they once maintained.

Ronin paused to brush Danielle's hair from her cheek. She was holding him back, despite the warm quivering of her inner walls, and he searched her body language for a reason. Bashful and blushing, Danielle asked, "Can I be on top?" He nodded his response, withdrew, and eased himself onto his knees between her calves.

She had to tuck her legs toward her chest and turn sideways to slide away from Ronin. Danielle smiled when she saw his attention drift down to her clean shaven pussy, and intentionally wiggled her buttocks on the bed to show off the thick bulge of flesh trapped between her inner thighs. Ronin moved back, waited for Danielle to clear a space, and then lowered himself onto his side facing the woman he'd found himself admiring more with each additional visit to his bedroom. "On top?" he asked politely and rolled onto his back.

For a moment it wasn't clear if Danielle was going to ride his chin or his cock.  Her heart thudded in her chest at the naughty desires that Ronin unleashed. On her knees, she straddled his waist, forced to spread her legs far apart and knowing her dripping pussy was on display for him, and then she lowered her sex down until Ronin's throbbing cock nudged against her inner thigh before being pressed against her swollen and sore labia.

Enjoying the way Ronin's wet erection glided over her lips, Danielle tipped her head back and savoured the ease of mounting and pushing down on him.  Her red hair flowed over her shoulders and her lily white neck was completely exposed - presenting a perfect portrait of her pale beauty while Danielle humped Ronin's cock with deep satisfaction.  She whispered to the ceiling, speaking to the sound of her own voice, saying, "...a gaping hole.  What I wanted."

Ronin's hands brushed over Danielle's ribs, and she lifted them to cradle the soft curve of her breasts. He massaged and kneaded the sensitive underside of her tits, and Danielle found a steady rhythm that guided Ronin's cock head into a good spot while enjoying his touch.  Her pussy drooled juices all over Ronin's pelvis.  Danielle clenched her buttocks, felt Ronin's cock jump within her, and her inner thighs slid against one another.  She was seeping so much wetness that her cunt lips were paint brushes that applied a generous coating to everything they came in contact with.

"Is this..." she hesitated and looked down at him. Ronin was comfortable and enjoying himself.  "It is good, isn't it?" His slow smile was all Danielle needed to see. Rocking side to side, she spread her legs further apart and settled her pelvis on to his. His scrotum pushed firmly against the bottom of her labia.

"It's very good," Ronin replied softly. He could see another emotional storm front coming, and it was clear that Danielle was still adjusting to what she had done. Ronin considered how so many women defined themselves by the size of their pussy. How so many women believed their best sexual asset was tightness and difficult entry. It had been a barrier between him and some women before. A specific woman was unavoidable in his mind. Now he watched as Danielle began exploring a whole different set of sensations and faced her widening awareness. All while he knew the conflicting doubts and beliefs that fought the intimate modifications of her sex wouldn't vanish over night.

It seemed to come out without conscious thought. Danielle almost bit the words back, but they were said. "What should I fuck now?" It wasn't really about fucking. It wasn't really about her sex. It was something more.

Ronin reached around Danielle's torso with strong hands and coaxed her to lean forward and rest on top of his chest. Her red hair spilled over his chin and mouth, and they both had to pull it to the side so Ronin could speak. Comforting Danielle in a soft hug while her pussy still ground against his pulsing cock, Ronin murmured, "Whatever feels good for you. Whatever you enjoy. It's your choice. Always has been."

Words that would have felt like judgment or entrapment came across differently while breathing in and out with Ronin. She felt a slight pop when Ronin's glans was tugged free from her grasping cunt while slowly uncoupling from him, and Danielle curled up alongside the man who had opened her mind... and her body. His goatee had chaffed her soft skin again, and some drifting thought process within the recesses of her mind was wondering if lotion would reduce the irritation. There was a sense of lingering contentment being there, accepted and cared for, but Danielle wanted to understand something, and what she wanted to understand was much more difficult to pin down. She started and stopped several times before taking hold of Ronin's bicep and asking, "Why?"

There were no words to answer that overly broad question. Ronin rolled over onto Danielle and pinned her hands above her head. His knees pushed her legs apart, and he thrust into the spread petals of her labia without hesitation. When his cock bottomed out, his glans grinding deep into the elastic walls of Danielle's sex and his pelvis pressing labia to bone, he backed out and drove in again. One thrust after another. The impact of each pistoning blow bruised Danielle's inner thighs and pubis. His one hand held her pinned underneath him while Ronin's other hand supported his weight. After three thrusts, Danielle tucked her knees back and to the side to give Ronin easier access to plumb the depths of her cunt. After another five or six strokes, Danielle began clenching with her abdomen and deliberately grasping his cock inside her pussy while pushing back at Ronin's pelvis.

He increased his pace, and the deep penetration started to stir and push Danielle's wetness from her pussy.  Her gaping cunt made wet sounds, and air flowed in and out of her hollow passage. Ronin kept going, and Danielle kept pushing back, and together they were building up to something more.  The intensity nudged Danielle onward, and she ignored all the little voices in her head and their customary objections to how Ronin fucked her.  It was truly fucking.  Not sex, not intercourse, not making love... fucking.

Ronin caught her ear, speaking low between controlled breaths, "This is why.  Why you came over.  Why you wanted to go further.  Why you wanted more. Why you-"

Danielle shushed him with a hiss.  "Why I asked you to turn my tight pussy into a gaping hole," she exhaled.  "Oh god... this feels..."  Her eyes fluttered while her vaginal walls trembled with a shuddering release.

He kept going.  Danielle's hands grabbed at the bed and the pillows, released from Ronin's grasp, and he continued pounding her sex.  Her wetness was a puddle spreading under her bare buttocks and running along her lower back while Ronin kept hammering into Danielle's overheated hole.  Danielle twisted and turned, her abs clenching and legs kicking, but Ronin pushed her onward.  He felt it before she understood what was happening, and pushed in close so his entire shaft was bathed in her fountaining release.

Shaking her head back and forth, hands clenching reflexively on air, Danielle tried to assert control over her body. Ronin moved from between her thighs and grabbed a towel, lifting Danielle's ass up for a moment to put it underneath her. He waited - slowly stroking Danielle's belly and arm - until she was able to breathe.

"What..." she was stammering, trying to form words with numb lips, while drifting in the afterglow.

Quietly Ronin caressed Danielle's cheek, unwittingly dabbing her own sex juices on her face, and said, "You squirted. It's pretty intense." He let her take his hand and watched while Danielle licked his fingers clean. "Did you know you could do that?" Ronin didn't hide the curiosity in his voice.

Danielle answered his silly question by reaching down and stroking her labia. Her gash was spread and open, engorged labia splayed to either sides of a slightly narrowing hole, and Danielle played with the lingering sensitivity and tension she encountered at the mouth of her pussy. It seemed to take effort to turn her head and focus on Ronin, but the redhead managed it and then tasted her own fingers again.

They shared another moment. Then Danielle slumped into the pillows and spoke to the ceiling fan above them, "I've always liked my taste." She grinned while sensing Ronin's wicked smile without even looking. "You've been so busy turning my pussy into a cunt and gaping hole that you never asked what I enjoy."

He ran a hand over his receding hairline, massaging his scalp while very aware that his heart was still recovering from the hard fucking he gave Danielle, and asked, "Any other secrets?" Ronin needed a break even though he hadn't cum yet.

Testing her way, Danielle rolled onto her side to face him. There was weakness there - something Danielle had never seen in Ronin before. His tenderness and caring, covered up by gruff words and harsh sentiments, was something Danielle had come to expect in Ronin's home. But now he was exposed, and Danielle wondered about it while reaching out to touch him. "Sometimes a kiss and a hug... make everything better..." She took his hand and lifted it to her mouth, gave Ronin a demure peck, and then set it down on her breast. "Sometimes you give everything... and you have nothing left for yourself..." The redhead moved closer to Ronin and felt the heat radiating from his body. With a gentle kiss on his cheek, and a graceful dalliance with his lingering hard-on, Danielle asked her question again but with different meaning. "What should I fuck now?" Her wink made it perfectly clear that she was open to anything Ronin suggested.

"More..." he murmured and relaxed. Danielle's hands moved over his chest, playing with the curls of brown hair, and then cupped his cock and scrotum.

"What should I fuck with my gaping hole?" Danielle teased. She explored the scars on the underside of Ronin's shaft, gliding over his juice soaked flesh, and tripping into the deep texture of his nut sack. "What would you like to see me fuck?" Danielle moved her fingers to Ronin's glans and caressed the underside of his cock head. His response was fading with his erection - Ronin was sinking into the bed's embrace and his breathing was deliberately slow and measured. Danielle moved down, pulling the towel with her so she didn't leave a slick trail on the sheets, and lowered her mouth to Ronin's cock. His neatly trimmed pubic hair had just enough bristle to scratch her chin while Danielle swallowed his cock head and worked her way halfway down the length of his shaft.

"Very few things..." Ronin murmured. He had to lift her head up to be heard. "Very few things we put in our mouths that we don't eventually bite."

His concern made Danielle smirk. He'd complained about her tight pussy, and now he was fussing about the size of her mouth. With deliberate practice, Danielle wrapped her tongue around his member and sucked his cock. Then she lifted off and kissed and licked her juices from the base of his shaft and scrotum. When she was done, Danielle could feel the wet mess on her face, and she let Ronin see it as well before using the towel to wipe off her mouth and chin. "I like to clean up. Tasting you and me together." She stretched out alongside Ronin. "But there wasn't much of you."

While Ronin focused on her body, Danielle

reached around her buttock and let her fingers follow the cleft of her ass to her anus. "Maybe the problem is that you need something more tonight." Two fingers, using her own tacky wetness, pushed at her tight sphincter. "But you can't stretch my bottom. I want it nice and tight." Eyes closed, Danielle moaned while her fingertips entered her ass. "I want to enjoy the difference... want to be able to play with myself... and feel it..." With a pained smile, Danielle met Ronin's brown eyed gaze. "I finger my ass all the time. And now... god... it feels so different from my cunt." Her knowing glance at Ronin's reinvigorated penis was all they needed to acknowledge his desire.

He moved slowly and let Danielle adjust herself on her back with her fingers in her ass. And then he pushed her legs up and fed his semi-erect cock into her cunt. There was no resistance, just the folds of her labia being brushed aside, and then Danielle felt his stiffening shaft grinding against her knuckles. "So I get to play with the gaping cunt..." he whispered.

"And I will finger my ass so I can enjoy both being open and being tight..." Danielle responded breathlessly.

Ronin's cock throbbed and jerked within her, and Danielle pushed her fingers deeper despite the strain on her wrist. It was an awkward duet, but they both were imagining how much better it would become with practice. Just one more thing Danielle could enjoy with Ronin.

Danielle and Ronin's story begins with "Intensity (The Complete Five Part Series) featuring Danielle," continues with "Satisfaction (The Complete Five Part Series) featuring Danielle," and "Submission (The Complete Five Part Series) featuring Danielle," and will include additional stories in future titles.

# Cherish Desire Creators

## Our Creators

Cherish Desire works with amazing skilled and experienced writers, editors, narrators, video narrators, models, photographers, musicians, and muses to create written, audio, and video content along with the supporting graphics, trailers, and music clips. While Max tackles the majority of assembling their contributions into a finished format, Cherish Desire would be a lot less without their involvement.

## Max

Max is the guy who walks into the war room on Saturday morning, black tight fitting Under Armour shirt beneath his buttondown shirt, and listens as developers, project managers, infrastructure leads, database admins, cloud admins, and deployment architects argue over hows and whys concerning a multimillion dollar solution effort that was supposed to go live months before. And then he's rearranging the puzzle pieces. Calling upon the people who need to be heard. Challenging the assumptions of execs with facts about real limitations and boundaries. Identifying on a whiteboard numerous pieces forgotten in the mad rush to get something launched. Throughout all that, the tension and hostility in the room grows, and he's the lightning rod for any number of people suddenly realizing they're on the hook for ridiculous amounts of effort before Monday morning. Yet he's the go to guy in these situations. Thinking faster than anyone else, leveraging the multi-disciplinary teams, and firefighting as he goes. Where did you think "an unrestrainable phenomena orthogonal to the Zeitgeist" came from? Max has always been forced to deal with megacorps across three continents, and it's no surprise he vents about it within stories that talk about real people instead of focusing on why he was traveling to cities across North American and Europe in the first place.

*This is definitely an unofficial and unauthorised blurb.* Here's a little bit more since you've read this far.

So much happens over the phone, in Zoom or Teams, and in emails now. So much has changed in how massive undertakings are orchestrated and executed. Even before the pandemic hit, fewer and fewer large corporations were willing to pay for consultants to travel onsite. And what would onsite even mean? Banks with half a dozen data centers in as many cities due to acquisitions. Insurers with the same. Healthcare providers and insurers rolled up into massive office centers in a few cities but operations throughout numerous states and regions. Auto manufacturers that divide centers of excellence across different countries to take advantage of lower salary and overhead costs. Consulting firms which own property used as distributed on demand office space to avoid needing to divest investments if they get pulled into auditing work.  There is no one site to be.  No one place where everyone critical to success and the adjacent stakeholders are at.

And that world changed within his lifetime. Which means it's personal.  The big burly Programme Manager who has utterly abdicated his responsibilities for six months tries to swoop in and attack Max for identifying deficiencies directly tied to exec mismanagement.  Not that Max said it that way, but the Programme Manager knows how it will be heard and discussed in the board room.  Everyone is anxious and agitated, looking away or fussing with their VPN tokens and notepads, or trying to invisibly type "OMG" on instant messenger on their laptop. Max only adjusts the angle of his gaze when the six foot plus tall Programme Manager stands up, stabbing a meaty hand at Max while towering over him from across the table, and waits until the explosive tirade ends.  He's devoid of emotion when he replies, "So we agree then.  You should have read the emails and summaries about these problems sent you to weekly for three months and actually done something about it."  Without bothering to wait for a response, Max turns to the Deployment Manager and begins talking about mitigation and remedies for packaging issues, asking for resources to work with developers so proper notes are made on how code was migrated to each environment, and the big man is left awkwardly standing and wondering what just happened to him before storming out of the room.

People who only know Max from the clubs, from

festivals, and from his weekends away from the madness should be forgiven for tuning out his boring monologues about worklife. It's difficult to listen to, full of jargon, and Max is a survivor of world changing initiatives, so he's seen things that most other consultants won't even come across much less have to deal with. All that, every bit of it, is very present when he writes about Tom and Ronin though. It's fundamental to their dualism and aggregate identity.

At some point, in some city, Max must have realized he was seeing things in a way others couldn't. That he needed mutually exclusive skillsets to deal with the various personalities thrust at him. That people were resources to be leveraged as well as obstacles to be overcome. That, with the right understanding of them, he could arrange things so those people were net contributors while acknowledging that meant they would also always consume some level of energy invested in making that happen. That there was no point in resenting the overhead of managing people if that overhead created opportunity and led to better outcomes.

And many years later, he wrote it out.

Just like his acquaintances from clubs and festivals are blind to the entirety of Max, I doubt his corporate colleagues see more than a fraction of him. He probably feeds them the appearances they anticipate, acts out the roles asked at him, and only adds enough of a twist that they realize something is happening in their peripheral vision. Something they take for granted after a short while but is very singularly Max in action. Ah. The black Under Armour shirt. He got pulled into the hallway of this dusty old adapted historical building in Greensboro, pulled out of the meeting he was effectively running for lack of anyone else capable of doing so, by that angry Programme Manager holding up a mobile phone on speakerphone. It was their director. After an explicative filled tirade which we couldn't not overhear, Max said calmly, "Get on a plane and tell me that to my face. Or realize that if I walk out of this building in the next five minutes and fly home then you and your bully are going to be dealing with an internal and client audit which will expose innumerable issues raised by me since I inherited this project from you both." We thought there was going to be a showdown. All we heard next was "Take me the fuck off speakerphone right now!"

Max didn't leave for long. He returned to the war room half an hour later with donuts, but he wasn't wearing his buttondown shirt any longer. We'd heard the Programme Manager taking multiple phone calls, desperately defending himself and blaming everyone except himself, and it all seemed pretty grim. When Max came back, he looked at all of us buried in emails on our laptops, shook his head, and asked what the revised deployment plan was. As if we should have been working on that all along – which I guess we should have – and his immediate launch into normalcy shook us all out of our stupor. It wasn't until later, in the afternoon after he sent the Programme Manager away to bring lunch to the war room, that I realized we were all roaring along to get shit done because Max was there.  Because we could see some part of him which he had hinted at but never exposed before.  Because we understood what had happened earlier was an ambush, and Max had worn that Under Armour shirt for a reason.

The way I figure it, there are men, like that Programme Manager, who are the size of bulls, built like oxen, and have always used their extreme physical presence to bully and intimidate others.  Given Max's long career, he'd run into that all over the world.  Those same men are never held accountable, are never to blame, and will destroy or sacrifice anyone on a whim.  I suppose Max knew that, too.  So the entire explosion, the insanity of attacking Max in front of his team and client leadership, and the easily overheard shouting at Max in the hallway from both the Programme Manager and his Director was way too predictable.  Max came to that fight emptyhanded, with only the facts as a shield, or so the Programme Manager must have thought.  And then Max came back with donuts to subtly apologize to the rest of us for being included in a fight which could not be avoided.  And wearing that tight fitting black Under Armour shirt which did nothing to cover how his torso, shoulders, and biceps flexed as he considered each person speaking, as he responded without raising his voice, and as he helped us think out loud about optimal approaches and collaborated with us on how to make everything come together.

Max never needed to be the bully in the room.  He never needed to intimidate us per se.  He just needed to make it painfully obvious that he was one hundred percent the wrong target for aggression and discontent.   That despite his studied emotional distance, his musculature conveyed a very different message.   He was more than capable of being whatever nightmares we could possibly imagine.  He was more than capable of being destructive and aggressive.   He was more than capable of being whatever he intended to be.  And he was unhappy, but we would get through this together.  Because it was the only way any of us could get out of that room *alive*.  He made that decision, to convey a message but to keep things civil, at the same time that his own management team were too emotional to do the same.  And some decisions change everything.

Maybe yours did as well.

# Cherish Desire Erotica

## Very Dirty Stories

We wanted to share our favorite sex stories.  The ones that broke out of the conventional erotica mold, shattered the limitations of casual romance and sex, and dove into detailed and realistic action involving stretching, large sex toy play, vaginal and anal fisting, domination, fantasy monster and animal dildo play, restraints and suspension, elaborate medical and DIY devices, and more.  We did it bit by bit, discovering and learning as we went, and released volume after volume of two to five short stories to challenge readers to be sexually aroused by something truly intense or charmingly subtle.  Very Dirty Stories volumes are about ladies that expose themselves and embrace their fears and desires as well as the men and women that inspire them to sexual peaks while living out wild sexual fantasies.

## Singles

We wanted to publish sexual adventures that were more than a one night stand.  So we gathered together our favorite ladies and delightfully sexy themes and created Singles - longer collections of sexual stories that fit together to cover formative physical and psychological experiences that define her womanhood or establish a collection of deviant delights and sexual alternatives. These trailblazing erotica books go deeper, harder, faster, and expose the soft white underbelly of sensual need while delivering thrust after thrust of sexual intensity and the soothing pleasures of passionate affection. Explore the explicit erogenous zones of women and their sexual partners. Be prepared for sexually challenging situations as well as character details that get beyond height, weight, hair colour, and favorite size of dildo. Plunge into their stories and get wet. Singles also make great gifts for that secret someone who needs a sexual swift kick in the nuts or a perverse surprise stashed for long trips and evenings in.

# ~~Very~~ Wicked Dirty Stories

The darkness of desires are shadows always encircling the hope of fulfillment and pleasure. These are the twisted realities fueled by the uninhibited passions and believes of the few. Their sexual urges, their powerful alliances, and their willingness to defend their own as well as to strike out and forcefully embrace what they require. ~~Very~~ Wicked Dirty Stories hint at the unobserved and strange frayed edges of reality that we like to censor or ignore. Ghosts, shapeshifters, and great powers linger just beyond the firelight while watching humanity sleep.

# Divinations

Cherish Desire Divinations erotica delves into darkness. Lusty shapeshifters, impassioned spirits, dangerous players, and perverse pagan deities beckon with sordid promises and unseemly urges. Their intense passions expose their bestial and heavenly natures while emphasizing how closely they represent unfettered hunger, cunning, love, and wickedness. Divinations was born of fevered imaginations and sexual abandonment that left us aching, bruised, and hoping for more. Divination books are collections of erotic stories that go deep and explore psycho-sexuality as well as physical modifications suited to the nearly immortal. The limited disguise of humanity has been stripped away, and the results are animalistic sexual rituals and self-enlightened spirituality that arouse jaded desires for more.

*Cherish Desire apologizes in advance for exposing the true nature of shapeshifters and the transcendent hungers that lurk behind every door and under every bed.*

# Discover More

For our complete catalog of titles, explore our books: https://wulf.fun/CherishDesireErotica

For more about your favorite characters, check out the ladies: https://wulf.fun/CherishDesireLadies

Very Dirty Stories, ~~Very~~ Wicked Dirty Stories, Cherish Desire Singles, and Cherish Desire Divinations titles include over 450 erotica stories to delight even the most jaded readers. With a focus on perverse desires that push limits to achieve blissful pleasure, intense action and taboo desires inspire fantasies and arousal for a satisfying climax.

The majority of Cherish Desire titles are available in digital editions with audio, video narration, and paperback editions for select stories and books.

And when you visit the Cherish Desire Catalog, get elite and a free eBook from Cherish Desire by signing up for the inside track.